IN OUR TEENY TINY Matzah HOUSE

By Bill and Claire Wurtzel

APPLES & HONEY PRESS

I'm Kitzel.
I live with my family
in a teeny tiny matzah house.
It is so crowded and
noisy in here.

Mom

Dad

Kitzel

Celeria

Zayde

Avo

Polly

I can't sleep in my favorite chair. Zayde got there first.

And I can't sleep under the chair because he snores so loudly. How can I dream about balls of yarn with all that noise over my head?

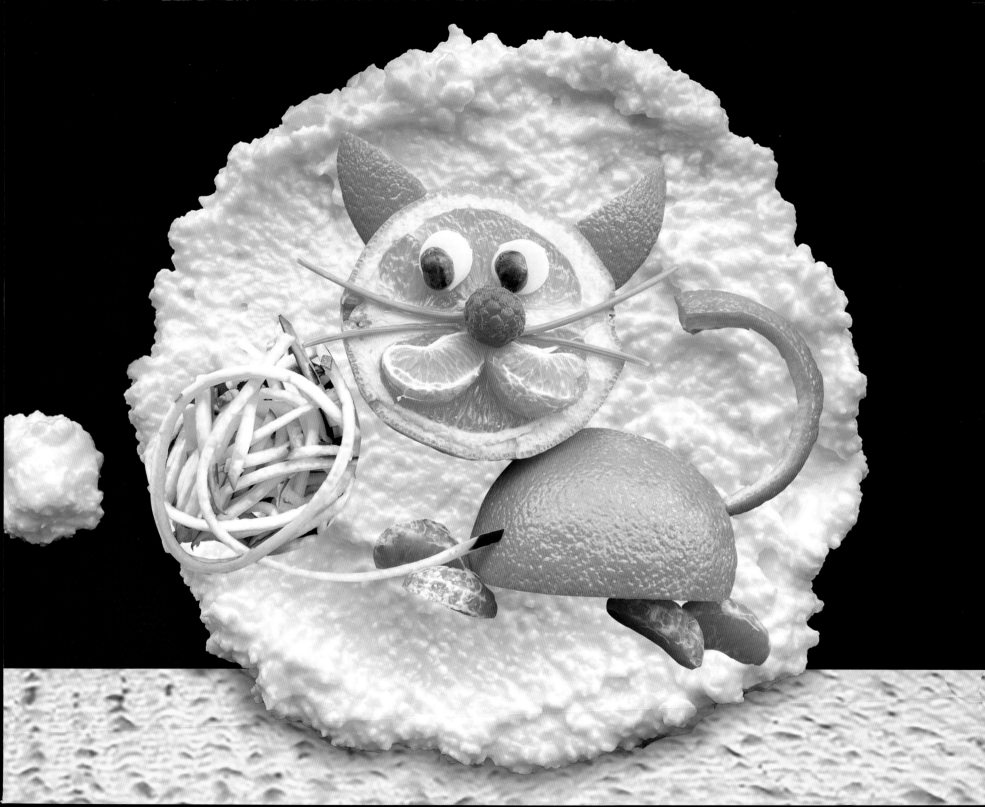

In our teeny tiny matzah house there's not enough room for Avo to play drums.

He plays anyway.

BOOM BO BOOM BOO

Dad complains he can't hear himself think.

And I can't hear myself meow.

In our teeny tiny matzah house, there's no room for Celeria to do her backflips.

Mom wonders, "Where are we going to put all our guests for the Passover seder?"

"AWWK!
It's too crowded here for a seder!"

"Oops, sorry Mom."

We have to get the house ready for Passover and say goodbye to bread.

"Bye, we'll be back in about a week."

Family and friends travel lots of different ways to come to our seder.

So many guests! How will everyone fit in our teeny tiny matzah house?

Some people join us remotely.

My friend Matzy joins in too.

Gefiltey

Mr. & Mrs. Matzowitz

Matzy

Souperman

Matzahballo

Moe & Minnie Matzahmealo

Cantor Loupe

Flankenella

Macaroony

Mat Zahbrei

Finally the seder begins.
Mom and Dad light the
candles and say blessings.

The table is so crowded that Celeria can show only three of the ten plagues.

Keep that wild beast
away from me!

Everyone sings Dayeinu.

DA-DAYEINU,

DA-DAYEINU,

DA-DAYEINU,

The kids run all over the place
looking for the afikoman.

I lend them a helping paw.

Finally, it's time for
the guests to go home.

They were having so much fun,
I thought they would never leave.

"Me three."

"I loved this seder."

"Me too."

"See y'all next Passover."

After Passover, our matzah house seems so big and quiet.

Holy cats, I have room to stretch out and take a nap.

Zzzz Zzzz Zzzz

Even with Avo playing all his drums and Zayde snoring.

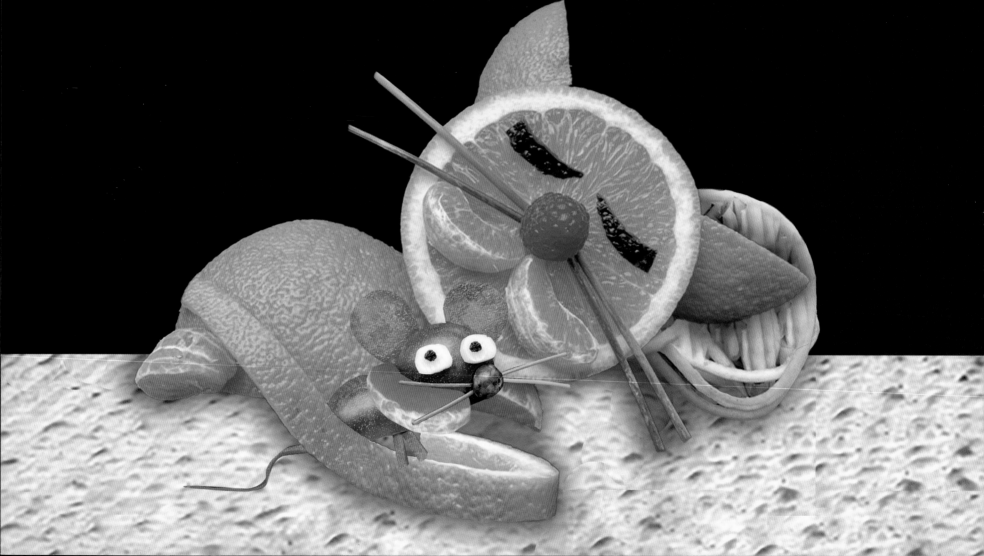

How to make your own Kitzel

1.

2.

3.

4.

5.

6.

7.

8.

9.

I dedicate this book to Bill, who keeps me laughing as he transforms our meals into hilarious characters.   — Claire

Thank you to Claire, our daughters Lisa and Nina, and our grandchildren, Ethan, Simon, and Daniela,
for encouraging my art and eating it too.   — Bill

Artist's note: I get my ideas from seeing the shapes and colors of different foods.
Then I let my imagination run wild and try to surprise myself.

Apples & Honey Press
An Imprint of Behrman House Publishers
Millburn, New Jersey 07041
www.applesandhoneypress.com

ISBN 978-1-68115-585-2

Library of Congress Control Number: 2021943550

Design by Alexandra N. Segal
Edited by Dena Neusner
Printed in China

1 3 5 7 9 8 6 4 2

0323/B2139/A3